A WEEK IN THE LIFE

OF BEST FRIENDS

A Week in the Life of Best Friends

and other poems of friendship

by Beatrice Schenk de Regniers
illustrated by Nancy Doyle

ATHENEUM   *New York*   1986

Atheneum
Macmillan Publishing Company
866 Third Avenue, New York, NY 10022

Type set by Linoprint Composition, Inc., New York City
Printed and bound by Maple-Vail Printing Company,
Binghamton, New York
Designed by Nancy Doyle and Mary Ahern

10   9   8   7   6   5   4   3   2   1

Library of Congress Cataloging-in-Publication Data

De Regniers, Beatrice Schenk.
A week in the life of best friends.

SUMMARY: A collection of poems describing some of
the joys and sorrows of friendship.
1. Friendship—Juvenile poetry.   2. Children's
poetry, American.   [1. Friendship—Poetry.   2. American
poetry]   I. Doyle, Nancy, ill.   II. Title.
PS3554.E1155W44   1986   811'.54   85-28680
ISBN 0-689-31179-6

for my best friend, francis
BdR

A WEEK IN THE LIFE

OF BEST FRIENDS

A WEEK IN THE LIFE OF BEST FRIENDS

On Monday
we swore,
Isabelle and I,
to be best friends forevermore.

On Tuesday
we agreed
to write each other notes
in secret code
that only *we* could read.

Wednesday
was the day we chose
secret sister-names.
(I can't tell you what they were.)
That same night
we 'phoned each other
to make sure
that
Thursday
both of us would wear
bows
of blue velvet in our hair.

On Thursday
we got the giggles—
tried to quit.
We couldn't.
Teacher had a fit
and kept us after school.
We didn't care.
Isabelle came home with me.
We cut each other's hair—
just a *little* bit.

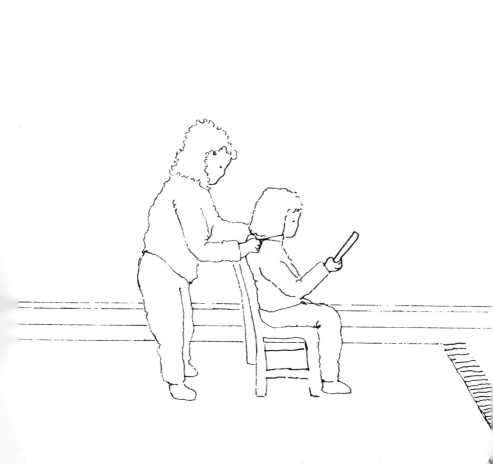

Friday,
the worst day of my life
(so far),
a new girl came to class.
And all the while that she was there,
she looked around her with a smile.
Her hair
was blow-cut in the latest style.
She looked just like a movie star.

Teacher told us that
the new girl's name was Arabelle.
Then she asked my best friend, Isabelle,
to be in charge of Arabelle
and show her where to go
and what to do.
So Isabelle
acted as if she had
a lot to do,
taking care
of Arabelle.
She didn't write a single note
to me.
And I was sure that she
didn't even read the one I wrote
to her (in code).

Then,
after school
Arabelle,
the louse,
invited Isabelle
to her house.

They whispered together.
Then Arabelle said to me,
out loud,
"Why don't you come too?"
"No, thanks.
I know when three's a crowd,"
I said,
and then went home and cried
and wished that I were dead.

Saturday,
I stayed in my room
the whole day long.
My mother said,
"What's wrong,
for goodness' sake?"

I said I had a stomach-ache
and what was more,
I sort of thought my throat was almost sore
and that my chest felt very tight
and that I thought I might
be getting
a fatal disease,
so would she please
leave me alone.

But then I told my mother
what really made me feel so bad
was that I no longer had
a best friend.

I told her all about Isabelle
and Arabelle,
and she said, well,
she thought she knew how I must feel,
but still
I shouldn't be so sure
that all was at an end,
that maybe I would like to call
my friend.

Just then the bell
rang. It was Isabelle!
All at once I felt quite well.

My mother let us pop some corn
and make mint tea
and cinnamon toast.
Isabelle said she liked me the most
of anyone she'd ever known,
and I no longer felt forlorn.

I said we ought
to start a secret club.
Isabelle said she thought
I should be president.
I said we could take turns.
She said OK.

Sunday,
we did our homework together.
then
we swore
again
to be best friends.

Now
it's four o'clock on Monday,
and we still
are best friends.
I think
we will
be,
evermore.

GOOD ADVICE

If your best friend's feeling tearful,
Try not to be too cheerful.
Just let her fill your ear full
    Of sad tales by the score.

And when she is through,
She'll feel as good as new.
Now *you'll* be feeling blue.
　　But that's what friends are for!

WHEN A FRIEND DIES

Did you ever have a dog?
I did.
And did it die?
Mine did.
And did you cry?
I did.

And do you know you never will
See him again alive and well?
I do.
But do you dream about him still
And love him more than you can tell?
I do.

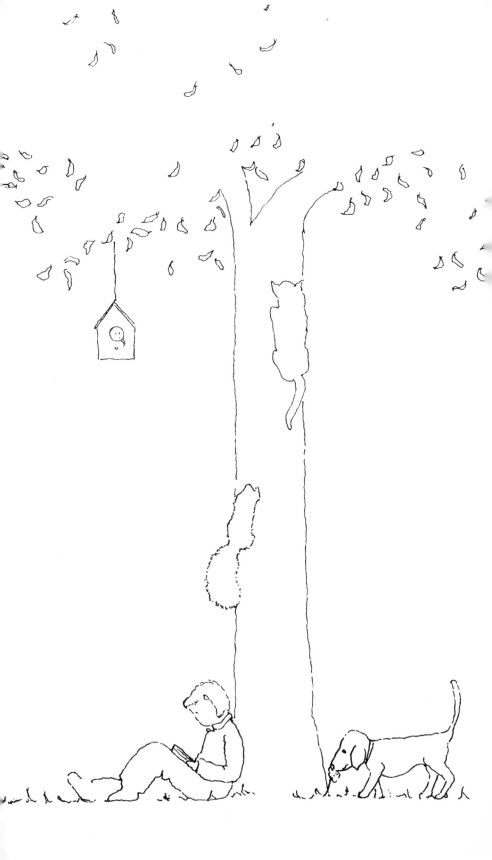

LET'S FACE IT

You can be
friend to a tree,
more or less—

You can strive
to keep it alive—
but in the end
you cannot truly say
the tree is your friend.

It is pleasant to be
in the shade of a tree.
But
I must say
though it may
cause you considerable annoyment,
that shade
isn't made
specifically for your enjoyment.

The tree doesn't care
who is there—
or who isn't.

CONSIDER THE BEE

The little boy
is eating breakfast in the garden
with his mother:

It is warm and sunny.
Bees are buzzing round and round.
"Bees are our friends," I hear him say.
"They give us honey."

"Oh, no!" His mother waves her hand
to shoo the bees away.
I see her shake
her head.
"You must understand
bees don't *give* us anything," she said.
"We *take*
honey from the bees!"

This answer didn't seem to please
the little boy.
I saw him frown.

He was quiet for a while.
At last he spoke:
"Well then," he said,
(and smiled a little smile
as though
he were smiling at a secret joke)
"I will be *their* friend instead."

And then and there
he dropped a bit of jam beside his plate
and watched a bee come round
and settle down
to share
his breakfast with him.

THERE ARE DAYS
AND THERE ARE DAYS

There are days I want to be
all alone
with only me
for company—
me and my cat.
There *are* days like that.

And there are days
(many more)
I don't want to be alone
any more.
Then
it seems to me
jokes are funnier,
honey's honey-er,
sun is sunnier
when
I'm with a friend!

BALLET IN THREE ACTS

I.

Alack!
My friend has left
and I'm bereft.

2.
Feeling better—
She sent a letter.

3.

Stars are singing,
Bells are ringing,
Flowers are blooming,
(No more glooming),
Bees are humming—
My friend is coming
                    back!

REPLY TO SOMEONE WHO ASKED WHY
THE TWO OF US ARE SUCH GOOD FRIENDS

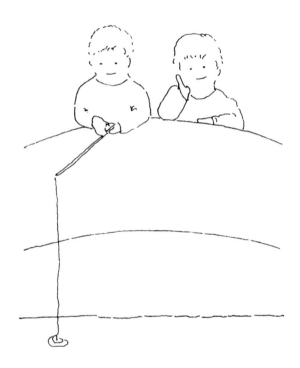

A friend doesn't have to be
Handsome or pretty.
We don't choose our friends
Just because they are witty.

My friend isn't perfect.
Others may be
Smarter or sweeter
Or nicer to me.

And sometimes we fight,
But that's quite all right—
—If we're mad in the morning,
We make up before night—
Because
    a friend
        is a friend
            is a friend.

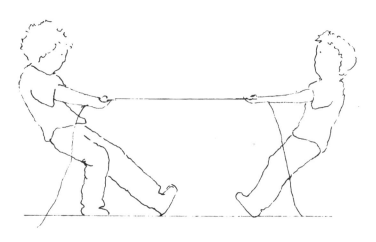

Why are we friends?
Don't ask us why.
We can't explain.
We won't even try.

Friends are not perfect.
They've plenty of flaws.
But that doesn't matter at all
Because
      a friend
            is a friend
                  is a friend.
So...

Whoever we are,
Whatever we be,
We're friends 'cause I'm I,
We're friends 'cause she's she.
(Or because he is he—
Whatever, whatever the case may be.)
    A friend
        is a friend
            is a friend!

A SECRET PLACE

I've found
a secret place today
high up on a hill.
The climb is steep.
The grass is deep.
No one can see me here.
But I can see the country
round about,
the river far below,
the hills and houses on the other side...

The only sound
here
is the wind
blowing through the trees.
Now a dog barks,
very far away.
There is no other person near.

I will come here every day
to read
or play
or just to hide.

And if I sit here very still
every kind of bug or insect will
come by.
They think that I'm part of the hill.

I can bring
a peanut butter sandwich here
and have a picnic.
Near-
by
blackberries grow,
bittersweet,
just right for birds
—and me—to eat.

This secret place is
oh, so fine—
and it's all mine!
My own secret nest.
Here I can hide
from everyone.
But in the end,
I wonder,
would it be more fun
if I shared the secret
with
my friend?
I can't decide...